THE GRAND INQUISITOR

FYODOR DOSTOYEVSKY

THE GRAND INQUISITOR
from The Brothers Karamazov

Translated by
David McDuff

penguin books

PENGUIN BOOKS

Published by the Penguin Group

Penguin Books USA Inc., 375 Hudson Street,
New York, New York 10014, U.S.A.
Penguin Books Ltd, 27 Wrights Lane,
London W8 5TZ, England
Penguin Books Australia Ltd, Ringwood,
Victoria, Australia
Penguin Books Canada Ltd, 10 Alcorn Avenue,
Toronto, Ontario, Canada M4V 3B2
Penguin Books (N.Z.) Ltd, 182–190 Wairau Road,
Auckland 10, New Zealand

Penguin Books Ltd, Registered Offices:
Harmondsworth, Middlesex, England

Published in Penguin Books 1995

Translation copyright © David McDuff, 1993
All rights reserved

This work is comprised of the chapters "The Mutiny" and "The Grand Inquisitor" from David McDuff's translation of *The Brothers Karamazov* by Fyodor
Dostoyevsky, published by Penguin Books.

ISBN 0 14 60.0115 X

Printed in the United States of America

Mutiny

'There is a certain confession I have to make to you,' Ivan began. 'I have never been able to understand how it is possible to love one's neighbour. In my opinion the people it is impossible to love are precisely those near to one, while one can really love only those who are far away. I once read somewhere concerning "Ioann the Almsgiver" (a certain saint) that when a hungry and frozen itinerant came to him and asked him to warm him, he put him to bed in his own bed, got into it together with him, put his arms around him and began to breathe into his mouth, which was festering and foul with some terrible disease. I'm convinced that he did this in the grip of a hysterical lie, out of a love that was prescribed by duty, and because of the *epithymia* he had taken upon himself. In order to love a person it is necessary for him to be concealed from view; the moment he shows his face—love disappears.'

'The Elder Zosima spoke of that on several occasions,' Alyosha observed. 'He also said that a person's face often prevents many who are as yet unpractised in love from loving him. But after all, there is much love in mankind, and it almost resembles the love of Christ, I myself know that, Ivan ...'

'Well I must say I *don't* at the present know it, nor do I

understand it, and there is a countless multitude of people who would go along with me there. The question is, of course, whether that's because of their inferior qualities, or whether it's just that their nature is so constituted. In my view, the love that Christ showed towards people is in its way a miracle impossible upon earth. It is true, he was God. But we are not gods. Let us assume, for example, that I suffer deeply—yet I mean, another person would never be able to perceive the degree to which I suffer, because he is another person, and not me, and on top of that it's seldom that a person will agree to recognize another as a sufferer (as though it were some kind of rank). Why won't he agree to it, do you suppose? Because, for example, I smell bad, or have a stupid expression on my face, or because I once trod on his toes. What's more, there is suffering and suffering: degrading suffering that degrades me—hunger, for example—is something that my benefactor will permit in me, but let the suffering be of ever such a slightly loftier sort, such as for an idea, for example, then no, only in very rare cases will he permit that, because he may, for example, look at me and suddenly perceive that the expression on my face is not at all like the one his fantasy supposes ought to be on the face of someone who is suffering for an idea. So he then at once deprives me of his beneficent deeds, though he does so not at all from any rancour of heart. Beggars, particularly beggars from good backgrounds, ought never to show themselves in public, but rather beg for alms through the medium of the newspapers. It's also possible to love one's neighbour in the abstract, and even sometimes from a distance, but almost never when he's close at hand. If things were always as they are on stage, at the ballet, where the beggars, when they appear, come on in silken rags and tattered lace and beg for alms while dancing gracefully, then one might still bring oneself to admire them. Admire, but not in any sense love. However, enough of that. I merely wanted to give you my point of view. I was going to go on to speak of the suffering of mankind in general, but let us rather concentrate on the sufferings of children. That will reduce the scope of my argument by some tenfold, but let us talk simply of children. Thus taking some of the wind out of my own sails, needless to say. Well, for one thing, young children may be loved even when they have ugly faces (though I think that young children never have ugly faces). And for another thing, I refrain from talking about grown-ups because, in addition to the fact that they are loathsome and do not deserve love, they also have requital for that: they have eaten of the apple and have grown aware of good and evil and become "as gods". They continue to eat it even to this day. But young children have not eaten of it at all and are as yet guilty of nothing. Are you fond of young children, Alyosha? I know that you are, and so you will understand why it is I want to talk of them at present. If they also suffer horribly upon earth, it is, of course, for their fathers, they are punished for their fathers who have eaten the apple—but, I mean, that is an argument from another world, one incomprehensible to the human heart here upon earth. It is out of the question that the innocent one shall suffer for another, especially when it is such an innocent as that! You may find it surprising in me, Alyosha, but I also am terribly fond of young children. And please take note that people who are cruel, enslaved by passion, carnivorous, Karamazovian, are sometimes very fond of children. Children, while they are children, until the age of seven, for example, are terribly apart from other people: it's as though they were a different species with a different nature. I knew a certain robber in prison: during his career he had had occasion, while massacring entire households in their homes, into which he broke at night in order to commit burglary, at the same time to murder several children, too. Yet, as he sat in prison, he grew fond of them to a degree that was strange. From a window of the gaol the only thing he did was watch the children playing in the prison yard. One small boy he taught to come and stand under the window where he was, and the boy became great friends with him ... You don't know why I'm saying all this, Alyosha? I seem to have a headache, and I feel sad.'

'You talk with a strange look,' Alyosha observed uneasily. 'It's as if you were in a kind of madness.'

'Incidentally, a certain Bulgarian I met in Moscow told me not so long ago,' Ivan Fyodorovich continued, almost without listening to his brother, 'about the atrocities committed by the Turks and Circassians down there in Bulgaria because of their fear of a mass uprising on the part of the Slavs—that is to say, burning, knifing, raping women and children, nailing convicts to fences by their ears and leaving them there until morning, when they hang them—and so on, it's not possible to imagine it all. Actually, people sometimes talk about man's "bestial" cruelty, but that is being terribly unjust and offensive to the beasts: a beast can never be as cruel as a human being, so artistically, so picturesquely cruel. The tiger simply gnaws and tears and that is the only thing it knows. It would never enter its head to nail people to fences by their ears and leave them like that all night, even were it able to do such a thing. Those Turks, by the way, even tormented children with voluptuous relish, from cutting them out of their mother's wombs with a dagger to throwing the babes in the air and catching them on bayonets before their mothers' eyes. The fact of it being before their mothers' eyes constituted the principal delight. There was, however, one small scene that interested me a great deal. Imagine: a mother stands trembling with an infant in her arms, around her the Turks who have entered. They contrive a merry little act: they fondle the infant, laugh in order to amuse it, they succeed, the infant laughs. At that moment a Turk points a pistol at it, four inches from its face. The baby boy laughs joyfully, stretches out his little hands to grab the pistol, and suddenly the artist pulls the trigger right in his face and smashes his little head to smithereens . . . Artistic, isn't it? As a matter of fact they say that Turks are very fond of sweet things.'

'Brother, where is all this leading?' Alyosha asked.

'I think that if the Devil doesn't exist and, consequently, man has created him, he has created him in his own image and likeness.'

'Just in the same way he created God, in that case.'

'Oh, you really do know how to turn the clever phrase, as Polonius says in *Hamlet*,' Ivan laughed. 'You beat me at my own game, good, I'm glad. After all, your God must be rather fine if man created him according to his own image and likeness. You asked just now why I was saying all these things: well, you see, one of my hobbies is the collecting of certain little facts; what I do, if you can credit it, is to note down and cull together from newspapers and reports, whatever the source, little anecdotes of a certain sort, and I now have a fine collection. The Turks are, of course, part of the collection, but they're all foreigners. I also have home-bred items which are even better that the Turkish ones. You know, with us it takes the form of flogging, the birch and the lash, and that is a national phenomenon: in our country the nailing of ears is unthinkable, we are Europeans, after all, but the rod and the lash—they are Russian, and cannot be taken away from us. In Europe it looks as though they have given up flogging altogether as a method of punishment, whether it's because their morals and manners have undergone a process of purification, or whether it's because laws have been established of such a kind that man may no more dare to flog his fellow man, but they have compensated themselves for that with another, as in our case, also purely national phenomenon, so national indeed that I think for us it would be impossible, though as a matter of fact it appears to be catching on among us too, in particular ever since the religious movement began to affect the higher levels of our society. I have in my possession a certain delightful little brochure, a translation from the French, which describes the execution in Geneva, by no means long ago, only some five years back, of a certain villain and murderer named Richard, a fellow of

6

twenty-three, I think, who repented and converted to the Christian faith upon the very scaffold. This Richard was someone's illegitimate son, who while yet a babe, about six years old, had been "given away" by his parents to some Swiss mountain shepherds, and they had nurtured him in order to employ him in labour. He grew up in their home like a small wild animal, the shepherds gave him no form of education but, on the contrary, when he was only seven sent him out to graze the flock, in the rain and cold, almost without clothing and almost without food. And then of course, so doing, not one of them reflected nor repented but, on the contrary, believed themselves fully within their rights, for Richard had been given to them like an object, and they did not even deem it necessary to feed him. Richard himself gave testimony that in those years he, like the Prodigal Son in the New Testament, would fain have filled his belly with the mash given to the pigs that were being fattened for sale, but he was not even given that and was flogged when he stole from the pigs, and thus he passed the whole of his childhood and youth until such time as he gained his maturity and, his energies fortified, embarked upon a life of petty thieving. The savage began to earn money by doing day labour in Geneva; he drank what he earned, lived like an outcast and ended by murdering some old man and robbing him. He was caught, put on trial and condemned to death. They don't have time for sentimentality over there, you know. Well, in prison he was at once surrounded by pastors and members of various Christian brotherhoods, charitable ladies and the like. In prison he was taught to read and write, had the New Testament explained to him, was exhorted, persuaded, pressured, pestered and weighed upon, and then lo and behold, in the end he himself solemnly confessed to his crime. He underwent conversion, he himself wrote to the court that he was a monster of cruelty and that at last he had been deemed worthy of being illumined by God and of receiving His grace. The whole of Geneva was in turmoil, the whole of pious and charitable Geneva. All who were of elevated station and good breeding rushed to see him in prison; Richard was kissed, embraced: "You are our brother, grace has come upon you!" And Richard himself only piously wept: "Yes, grace has come upon me! Before, all my childhood and youth, I would fain have eaten of the husks that the swine did eat, yet now grace has come upon me, and I die in the Lord!" "Yes, yes, Richard, die now in the Lord, you have shed blood and must die in the Lord. Even though you are not to blame for being wholly ignorant of the Lord at all at the time when you envied the swine their husks and when you were flogged for stealing their husks from them (which was a very bad thing to do, for stealing is not permitted), you have shed blood and must die." And then his last day arrived. The unnerved Richard wept and could do nothing but repeat every moment: "This is the finest day of my life, I am going to the Lord!" "Yes," cried the pastors, the judges and the charitable ladies, "this is your happiest day, for you are going to the Lord!" All these people made their way to the scaffold behind the cart of shame in which Richard was being taken there, in carriages, on foot. Then they attained the scaffold: 8 "Die now, brother," they cried to Richard, "die in the Lord, for grace has come upon you!" And then, covered in the kisses of his brothers, brother Richard was hauled to the scaffold, placed upon the guillotine and had his head lopped off in brotherly fashion, since grace had come upon him. Well, that's characteristic. This brochure was translated into Russian by some Russian Lutheran charity-mongers from the upper levels of society and distributed free of charge by the newspapers and other publishers for the enlightenment of the Russian people. The good thing about the Richard story is its national quality. Though in our country it seems to people absurd to cut off someone's head because he has become a brother to us and because grace has come upon him, we do none the less, I repeat, have our own such folly, one that is possibly even worse. In our country the torture of flogging is a historical, direct and most intimate source of pleasure. Nekrasov has some lines about a muzhik lashing his horse with a knout on the eyes, "on its meek eyes". Who has not seen such a thing, it is a *russisme*. He described a puny little horse, on whose cart too much has been piled, getting bogged down with its load, unable to haul it out. The muzhik flogs it, flogs it in a frenzy, flogs it, at last, not understanding what he is doing, in an intoxication of flogging lashes it viciously, countless times. "Though you are not strong enough, yet pull, even though it kills you, pull!" The wretched little jade strains, and then he starts to lash it, the defenceless creature, about its eyes, "its meek and weeping eyes". Beside itself it gives a jerk, hauls the cart out and sets off, trembling all over, not breathing, almost sideways, with a kind of hopping skitter, somehow unnaturally and ignominiously—in 9

Nekrasov that is terrible. But after all, it is only a horse, and God gave horses unto man that he might flog them. Or so at any rate the Tartars would have had us understand, giving us the knout as a reminder of it. But after all, human beings may be flogged, too. And so here we have a cultured gentleman of progressive education and his lady wife flogging their own daughter, a babe of seven years, with the birch—I have a detailed account of it noted down. The dear papa is glad the twigs have knots in them, "It will sting more", he says, and then he begins to "sting" his own daughter. I know for a certainty that there are floggers of a kind who grow excited with each blow to the point of voluptuous pleasure, quite literally voluptuous pleasure, increasingly with each consecutive blow, progressively. They flog for a minute, they flog for five, they flog for ten, onward, harder, faster, more and more painfully. The child cries out, the child is, at last, unable to cry out, it gasps: "Papa, papa, my papa, my papa!" By some devilish piece of bad luck the case is brought to court. An advocate is hired. The advocate was long ago characterized by the Russian people in the saying "the *ablakat* is a hired conscience". The advocate cries out in defence of his client. "The case," he says, "is such a simple one, so ordinary and based in family life—a father gives his daughter a thrashing, and to the shame of the times we live in is taken to court!" Persuaded, the members of the jury retire and bring back a verdict of not guilty. The members of the public roar with happiness that the torturer has been acquitted. I wasn't there, damn it, or I'd have bellowed a proposal that a stipend be founded in the torturer's name! . . . Delightful little scenes.

10

But I have even better ones concerning young children, I have a great, great many items about Russian children in my collection, Alyosha. The father and mother of a little five-year-old girl, "most respectable and high-ranking people, educated and of progressive views", conceived a hatred of her. Let me tell you, I once again positively assert that in many scions of mankind there is a curious property—the love of torturing children, but only children. To all other specimens of the human race these same torturers are even favourably and meekly inclined, as befitting humane men of European and progressive education, but they have a great love of torturing children, and their love for children is even based on that. It is the very unprotected aspect of these creatures that tempts the torturers, the angelic trustfulness of the child, which has nowhere to go and no one to turn to—this it is that excites the foul blood of the torturer. In every human being, of course, there lurks a beast, a beast of anger, a beast of voluptuous excitement derived from the cries of the tortured victim, a beast uncontrollable, unleashed from the chain, a beast of ailments contracted in debauchery—gout, cirrhosis and the like. Those progressively educated parents subjected that poor five-year-old girl to every torture one could think of. They beat her, flogged her, kicked her, themselves not knowing why, turned her whole body into a mass of bruises; at last they attained the highest degree of refinement: in the cold and freezing weather they locked her up for a whole night in the outside latrine because she did not ask to be relieved (as though a five-year-old child, sleeping its sound, angelic sleep, could learn to ask to be relieved at such an age)—what is more, they smeared her eyes, cheeks and mouth all over with faeces and compelled her to eat those faeces, and it was the mother, the mother who did the compelling! And that mother was able to sleep, hearing at night the moans of the poor little child, locked up in the foul latrine! So now do you understand, when a small creature that is not yet able to make sense of what is happening to it beats its hysterical breast in a foul latrine, in the dark and cold, with its tiny fists and wails with its bloody, meek, rancourless tears to "dear Father God" to protect it—now do you understand all that rot, my friend and my brother, my godly and humble lay brother, do you understand why all that rot is so necessary? Without it, they say, man would not be able to survive upon earth, for he would not know good from evil. Why recognize that devilish good-and-evil, when it costs so much? I mean, the entire universe of knowledge is not worth the tears of that little child addressed to "dear Father God". I say nothing of the sufferings of grown-ups— they have eaten the apple, and the devil with them, and the devil take them all, but the children, the children! I'm tormenting you, Alyosha, my lad, you look as though you were beside yourself. I shall stop, if you wish.'

'It's all right, I also want to suffer,' Alyosha muttered.

'Just one, just one more little scene, and that for curiosity's sake, a very characteristic one, and principally because I've just read about it in one of the symposia of our antiquities, either in the *Archive* or the *Antiquity*, I think; I'd have to check up, I've even forgotten where I read it. It happened

during the blackest period of serfdom, back at the start of the century, and all hail to the Liberator of the people! Back then at the start of the century there was a certain general, a general with grand connections, a most prosperous landowner, but of the sort (to be sure, even then it appears very few in number) who upon retiring from the service were very nearly convinced that they had earned the right to dispose over the lives and deaths of their subjects. In those days there were such men. Well, so the general lived on his estate of two thousand souls, swaggered around, treating his lesser neighbours as though they were his retainers and buffoons. A kennel with hundreds of dogs and nearly a hundred huntsmen, all in uniforms, all on horseback. And then one day a serf boy, a little lad of only eight years old, while playing some game or other threw a stone and bruised the leg of the general's favourite beagle. "Why has my favourite dog gone lame?" "It was the boy," he was informed, "he threw a stone at it and bruised its leg." "Ah, so it was you," the general said, looking him over. "Seize him!" He was seized, taken from his mother, kept overnight in the lock-up, and at first light the next morning the general came driving out in full dress-uniform, mounted his horse, around him his retainers, dogs, huntsmen, stalkers, all on horseback. Around them the serf folk were gathered for the purpose of edification, and in front of them all the mother of the guilty boy.

'The boy was brought out from the lock-up. A cold, gloomy, misty autumn day, first-rate for hunting. The general ordered the boy to be undressed, he was stripped naked, shivering, out of his mind with terror, not daring to utter a sound ... "Send him on his way!" the general ordered.

"Run, run!" the huntsmen shouted to him, the boy set off at a run ... "Tally ho!" the general howled and unleashed at him a whole pack of borzoi hounds. He hunted him down in front of his mother, and the dogs tore the child to shreds! ... I think the general was put in ward. But ... what should one have done with him? Shot him? Shot him in order to satisfy one's moral feelings? Tell me, Alyosha, my lad!'

'Shot him!' Alyosha said quietly, raising his eyes to his brother with a kind of pale, distorted smile.

'Bravo!' Ivan howled in a kind of ecstasy. 'Why, if you can say that, it means ... A fine schemonach you are! So that's the kind of little devil that crouches in your heart, Alyosha Karamazov, my lad!'

'It was a preposterous thing for me to say, but ...'

'There you have it—but! ...' Ivan shouted. 'You ought to realize, novice, that preposterous things are all too necessary upon earth. The world rests upon preposterous things, and indeed it's possible that without them absolutely nothing would ever have come into existence. We know that which we know!'

'What do you know?'

'That I don't understand anything,' Ivan continued in a kind of delirium. 'And that I don't want to understand anything now, either. I want to remain with the facts. I decided long ago not to understand. If I understand anything, I shall instantly be untrue to the facts, and I have decided to remain with the facts ...'

'Why are you putting me to the test like this?' Alyosha exclaimed in hysterical sorrow. 'Will you please finally tell me?'

'Of course I will, to tell you is what I've been leading up to. You are dear to me, and I don't want to let you go and shall not yield to your Father Zosima.'

Ivan said nothing for a moment, and his face suddenly became very sad.

'Listen to me: I took the exclusive instance of young children in order to make it more obvious. Of the other human tears in which the earth is steeped from crust to core I have not said a word, I have purposely kept my subject narrow. I am a bedbug and I confess with all due self-disparagement that I am quite unable to understand why everything is ordered thus. So it must be the fault of people themselves: given paradise, they wanted freedom and stole fire from heaven, knowing the while that they would be unhappy, and so there is no reason to feel sorry for them. Oh, with my pathetic, earthly, Euclidean mind I only know that there is suffering, that "none does offend", that one thing proceeds from another, quite plainly and simply, that everything flows and evens out—but after all, that is merely Euclidean rubbish, and after all, I know it, but I cannot agree to live by it! What is it to me that "none does offend" and that I know it? I want retribution, otherwise I shall destroy myself. And retribution not at some place and some time in infinity, but here upon earth, and in such a way that I see if for myself. I have believed in it, and I want to see it for myself, and if by that time I am already dead, then let me be raised up again, for if it all takes place when I am not there, it will be too hurtful. For I did not suffer in order with my villainous actions and my sufferings to manure a future harmony for someone else.

I want with my own eyes to see the lion lie down beside the fallow deer and the one who has been slaughtered get up and embrace the one who has killed him. I want to be here when everyone suddenly discovers why it has all been the way it has. All the religions of the earth have been founded on that desire, and I believe. But here, however, are the children, and what am I going to do with them then? That is the question I am unable to resolve. For the hundredth time I repeat—there are a great number of questions, but I have taken the sole instance of young children for here it is irrefutably evident what I must say. Look: if everyone must suffer in order with their suffering to purchase eternal harmony, what do young children have to do with it, tell me, please? It is quite impossible to understand why they should have to suffer, and why should they have to purchase harmony with their sufferings? Why have they also ended up as raw material, to be the manure for someone else's future harmony? Solidarity in sin among human beings I understand; I even understand solidarity in retribution, but I mean to say, there can be no question of solidarity in sin among young children, and if it is indeed true that they are solidary with their fathers in all the villainous actions of their fathers, then it goes without saying that therein is a truth that is not of this world and is impossible for me to understand. Some wag will perhaps say that, like it or not, the child will grow up and in time commit sins—but here is one who has not grown up and yet at eight years old was hunted down by dogs. Oh, Alyosha, I do not blaspheme! And I understand what a shaking must rend the universe when all that is in heaven and under the earth flows together in one laudatory voice and all that liveth and hath lived exclaims: "Just and true art Thou, O Lord, for Thy ways are made plain!" And when the mother embraces the torturer who tore her son to pieces with his dogs, and all three of them proclaim in tears: "Just and true art Thou, O Lord," then, of course, the day of knowledge will have dawned and all will be explained. The only trouble is that it's precisely that I cannot accept. And for as long as I am on the earth I shall hasten to make arrangements of my own. You see, Alyosha, it may very well be, perhaps, that when I reach the moment in my life at which I see it, or rise up from the dead in order to do so, I myself may exclaim with all the rest, as I watch the mother embracing the torturer of her little child: "Just and true art Thou, O Lord!", but it is something I do not want to do. While there is still time I shall hasten to guard myself, and so I decline the offer of eternal harmony altogether. It is not worth one single small tear of even one tortured little child that beat its breast with its little fist and prayed in its foul-smelling dog-hole with its unredeemed tears addressed to "dear Father God"! It is not worth it because its tears have remained unredeemed. They must be redeemed, or there can be no harmony. But by what means, by what means will you redeem them? Is it even possible? Will you really do it by avenging them? But what use is vengeance to me, what use to me is hell for torturers, what can hell put right again, when those children have been tortured to death? And what harmony can there be where there is hell: I want to forgive and I want to embrace—I don't want anyone to suffer any more. And if the sufferings of children have gone to replenish the sum of suffering that was needed in order to purchase the truth, then I declare in advance that no truth, not even the whole truth, is worth such a price. And above all, I do not want the mother to embrace the torturer who tore her son to pieces with his dogs! Let her not dare to forgive him! If she wants, she may forgive him on her own account. She may forgive the torturer her limitless maternal suffering; but as for the sufferings of her dismembered child, those she has no right to forgive, she dare not forgive his torturer, even if her child himself forgave him! And if that is the case, if they dare not forgive, where is the harmony? Is there in all the world a being that could forgive and have the right to forgive? I do not want harmony, out of a love for mankind I do not want it. I want rather to be left with sufferings that are unavenged. Let me rather remain with my unavenged suffering and unassuaged indignation, *even though I am not right*. And in any case, harmony has been overestimated in value, we really don't have the money to pay so much to get in. And so I hasten to return my entry ticket. And if I am at all an honest man, I am obliged to return it as soon as possible. That is what I am doing. It isn't God I don't accept, Alyosha, it's just his ticket that I most respectfully return to him.'

'That is mutiny,' Alyosha said quietly, his eyes lowered.

'Mutiny? I don't like to hear you say such a word,' Ivan said with emotion. 'One can't live in a state of mutiny, but I want to live. Tell me yourself directly, I challenge you— reply: imagine that you yourself are erecting the edifice of human fortune with the goal of, at the finale, making people

18

happy, of at last giving them peace and quiet, but that in order to do it it would be necessary and unavoidable to torture to death only one tiny little creature, that same little child that beat its breast with its little fist, and on its unavenged tears to found that edifice, would you agree to be the architect on those conditions, tell me and tell me truly?'

'No, I would not agree,' Alyosha said quietly.

'And are you able to allow the idea that the people for whom you are constructing the edifice would themselves agree to accept their happiness being bought by the unwarranted blood of a small, tortured child and, having accepted it, remain happy for ever?'

'No, I cannot. Brother,' Alyosha said suddenly, his eyes flashing, 'just now you said: "Is there in all the world a Being that could forgive and have the right to forgive?" Well, that Being does exist, and It can forgive everything, everyone, man and woman alike, *and for everything*, because It gave its innocent blood for all things and all men. You have forgotten about It, but on It the edifice is founded, and this it is that people will exclaim to It: "Just and true art Thou, O Lord, for Thy ways are made plain." '

'Ah, you mean "the only sinless one" and His blood! No, I haven't forgotten about Him and have, on the contrary, been amazed at how long it has taken you to introduce Him into the argument, for your kind usually wheel Him out right at the start. Listen, Alyosha, don't laugh, but I once composed a *poema*—I did it about a year ago. If you're able to waste another ten minutes or so with me, would you let me tell you what it says?'

'You've written a *poema*?'

'Oh, no, I didn't write it,' Ivan said, laughing, 'never in my life have I written down so much as two lines of verse. No, I dreamed this *poema* up and committed it to memory. I dreamed it up with passion. You shall be my first reader, or listener, rather,' Ivan said with an ironic smile. 'Shall I tell you what it says or not?'

'By all means,' Alyosha managed to get out.

'My *poema* is entitled "The Grand Inquisitor", a preposterous thing, but I feel like telling it to you.'

The Grand Inquisitor

'You see, even here we can't get by without a preface—a literary preface, that is, confound it!' Ivan said, laughing. 'And what kind of an author am I? Look, the action of my poem takes place in the sixteenth century, and back then—as a matter of fact, this ought still to be familiar to you from your days at school—back then it was the custom in works of poetry to bring the celestial powers down to earth. Dante I need hardly mention. In France the magistrates' clerks and also the monks in the monasteries used to give entire dramatic spectacles in which they brought on to the stage the Madonna, the angels, the saints, Christ and even God Himself. Back in those days it was all very unsophisticated. In Victor Hugo's *Nôtre Dame de Paris*, under the reign of Louis

XI, an edifying spectacle is given to the people free of charge in the auditorium of the Paris Town Hall, to celebrate the birthday of the French Dauphin, under the title *Le bon jugement de la très sainte et gracieuse Vièrge Marie*, in which she herself appears in person and pronounces her *bon jugement*. In our own country, in the Moscow of pre-Petrine antiquity, dramatic spectacles of almost the same kind, especially of stories from the Old Testament, also took place from time to time; but, in addition to dramatic spectacles, there passed throughout all the world a large number of tales and "verses" in which when necessary the saints, the angels and all the powers of heaven wrought their influence. The monks in our monasteries also occupied themselves with the translation, copying and even the composition of such poems, and in such times, too: under the Tartar yoke. There is, for example, a certain little monastic poem (from the Greek, of course) entitled *The Journey of the Mother of God Through the Torments*, with scenes and with a boldness that are not inferior to those of Dante. The Mother of God visits hell, and her guide through the "torments" is the Archangel Michael. She beholds the sinners and their sufferings. This hell, incidentally, contains a most entertaining category of sinners in a burning lake: those of them who sink into this lake so deep that they are unable to swim to its surface again are "forgotten by God"—a phrase of exceptional force and profundity. And lo, the shocked and weeping Mother of God falls down before God's throne and appeals to him to grant forgiveness to all who are in hell, all whom she has seen there, without distinction. Her entreaty with God is of colossal interest. She implores him, she will not depart, and when God draws her attention to the nailed hands and feet of His Son and asks her: "How can I forgive his torturers?" she commands all the saints, all the martyrs, all the angels and archangels to fall down together with her and pray for the forgiveness of all without discrimination. The upshot of it is that she coaxes from God a respite from the torments each year, from Good Friday to Whit Sunday, and out of hell the sinners at once thank the Lord and loudly cry unto Him: "Just and true art thou, O Lord, that thou hast judged thus." Well, my little poem would have been in similar vein, had it appeared in those days. He appears on my proscenium; to be sure, in my poem. He does not say anything, only makes his appearance and goes on his way. Fifteen centuries have now passed since He made his vow to come in his kingdom, fifteen centuries since his prophet wrote: "Behold, I come quickly." "But of that day and that hour knoweth no man, not even the Son, but only my Father in heaven," as He himself prophesied while yet on the earth. But human kind awaits him with its earlier faith and its earlier tender emotion. Oh, with even greater faith, for fifteen centuries have now passed since the pledges have ceased to be lent to man from the heavens:

> Thou must have faith in what the heart saith,
> For the heavens no pledges lend.

'And only faith in that which is said by the heart! To be sure, there were many miracles back in those days. There were saints who effected miraculous healings; to some righteous men, according to their life chronicles, the Queen of Heaven herself came down. But the Devil does not slumber, and in humankind there had already begun to grow a doubt in the genuineness of these miracles. Just at that time there appeared in the north, in Germany, a terrible new heresy. An enormous star, "burning as it were a lamp" (that's the church, you see), "fell upon the fountains of the waters, and they were made bitter." These heresies began blasphemously to contradict the miracles. But all the more ardent was the faith of those who remained true believers. The tears of humankind ascended to Him as before, He was awaited, loved, trusted in, people thirsted to suffer and die for him, as before ... And for how many centuries had humankind prayed with faith and ardour: "O God the Lord, show us light", for how many centuries had it appealed to Him that He, in His immeasurable compassion, should deign to come down among His supplicants. He had been known to condescend before and had visited certain men of righteousness, martyrs and holy cenobites while yet they lived on earth, as it is written in their "Lives". Among us Tyutchev, who believed profoundly in the truth of His words, announced that

> Weighed down by the Cross's burden,
> All of you, my native land,
> Heaven's Tsar in servile aspect
> Trudged while blessing, end to end.

Which really was the case, I do assure you. And so it happens that He conceives the desire to manifest Himself, if only 23 for an instant, to His people—to His struggling, suffering, stinkingly sinful people that none the less childishly love Him. My poem is set in Spain, at the most dreadful period of the Inquisition, when bonfires glowed throughout the land every day to the glory of God and

> In resplendent *autos-da fé*
> Burned the wicked heretics.

Oh, this is not, of course, that coming in which He will appear, according to His promise, at the end of days in the clouds of heaven with power and great glory and which will take place suddenly, "as the lightning cometh out of the east, and shineth even unto the west". No, He has conceived the desire to visit his children at least for an instant and precisely in those places where the bonfires of heretics had begun to crackle. In His boundless mercy He passes once more among men in that same human form in which for three years He walked among men fifteen centuries earlier. He comes down to the "hot streets and squares" of the southern town in which only the previous day, in a "resplendent *auto-da-fé*", in the presence of the king, the court, the knights, the cardinals and the loveliest ladies of the court, in the presence of the numerous population of all Seville, there have been burned by the Cardinal Grand Inquisitor very nearly a good hundred heretics all in one go, *ad majorem gloriam Dei*. He has appeared quietly, unostentatiously, and yet—strange, this—everyone recognizes Him. That could have been one of the best bits in my poem—I mean, the question of why it is that

24

everyone recognizes him. The people rush towards him with invincible force, surround him, mass around him, follow him. Saying nothing, He passes among them with a quiet smile of infinite compassion. The sun of love burns in his heart, the beams of Light, Enlightenment and Power flow from his eyes and, as they stream over people, shake their hearts with answering love. He stretches out His arms to them, blesses them, and from one touch of Him, even of His garments, there issues a healing force. Then from the crowd an old man, blind since the years of his childhood, exclaims: "O Lord, heal me, that I may behold thee," and lo, it is as though the scales fall from the blind man's eyes, and he sees Him. The people weep and kiss the ground on which He walks. The children throw flowers in his path, singing and crying to Him: "Hosannah!" "It's Him, it's Him," they all repeat, "it must be Him, it can't be anyone but Him." He stops in the parvis of Seville Cathedral just at the moment a white, open child's coffin is being borne with weeping into the place of worship: in it is a seven-year-old girl, the only daughter of a certain noble and distinguished citizen. The dead child lies covered in flowers. "He will raise up your child," voices cry from the crowd to the weeping mother. The cathedral *pater* who has come out to meet the coffin looks bewildered and knits his brows. But then the mother of the dead child utters a resounding wail. She throws herself at his feet: "If it is You, then raise up my child!" she exclaims, stretching out her arms to him. The procession stops, the coffin is lowered to the parvis floor, to his feet. He gazes with compassion, and his lips softly pronounce again: 25

"Talitha cumi"—"Damsel, I say unto thee, arise." The girl rises in her coffin, sits up and looks around her, smiling, with astonished, wide-open eyes. In her arms is the bouquet of white roses with which she had lain in the coffin. Among the people there are confusion, shouts, sobbing, and then suddenly, at that very moment, on his way past the cathedral comes the Cardinal Grand Inquisitor himself. He is an old man of almost ninety, tall and straight, with a withered face and sunken eyes, in which, however, there is still a fiery, spark-like gleam. Oh, he is not dressed in his resplendent cardinal's attire, the attire in which yesterday he showed himself off before the people as the enemies of the Roman faith were being burned—no, at this moment he wears only his old, coarse monkish cassock. Behind him at a certain distance follow his surly assistants and servants and the "Holy" Guard. He stops before the crowd and observes from a distance. He has seen it all, has seen the coffin being put down at His feet, has seen the damsel rise up, and a shadow has settled on his face. He knits his thick, grey brows, and his eyes flash with an ill-boding fire. He extends his index finger and orders the guards to arrest Him. And lo, such is his power and so accustomed, submissive and tremblingly obedient to him are the people that the crowd immediately parts before the guards, and they, amidst the sepulchral silence that has suddenly fallen, place their hands on Him and march Him away. Instantly, the crowd, almost as one man, bow their heads to the ground before the Elder-Inquisitor, and without uttering a word he blesses the people and passes 26 on his way. The Guard conduct the Captive to a narrow and

murky vaulted prison in the ancient building of the Ecclesiastical Court and lock Him up in it. The day goes by, and dark, passionate and "unbreathing" Seville night begins. The air "of lemon and of laurel reeks." In the midst of the deep murk the prison's iron door is suddenly opened and the old Grand Inquisitor himself slowly enters the prison with a lamp in his hand. He is alone, the door instantly locks again behind him. He pauses in the entrance and for a long time, a minute or two, studies His face. At last he quietly goes up to Him, places the lamp on the table and says to Him:

' "Is it you? You?" Receiving no answer, however, he quickly adds: "No, do not reply, keep silent. And in any case, what could you possibly say? I know only too well what you would say. And you have no right to add anything to what was said by you in former times. Why have you come to get in our way? For you have come to get in our way, and you yourself know it. But do you know what will happen tomorrow? I do not know who you are, and I do not want to know: you may be He or you may be only His likeness, but tomorrow I shall find you guilty and burn you at the stake as the most wicked of heretics, and those same people who today kissed your feet will tomorrow at one wave of my hand rush to rake up the embers on your bonfire, do you know that? Yes, I dare say you do," he added in heartfelt reflection, not for one moment removing his gaze from his Captive.'

'I don't quite understand this part of it, Ivan,' Alyosha smiled; all the time he had listened in silence. 'Is it simply an immense fantasy, or is it some mistake on the part of an old man, some impossible *quiproquo*?'

'Why don't you assume it's the latter.' Ivan burst out laughing. 'If you've been so spoiled by contemporary realism that you can't endure anything fantastic and you want it to be a *quiproquo*, then so be it. It certainly can't be denied,' he laughed again, 'that the old man is ninety, and might easily have long ago been driven insane by the idea that is in his mind. On the other hand, the Captive might have struck him by His appearance. Or it might simply have been a hallucination, the vision of a ninety-year-old man on the threshold of death, given added feverish intensity by the previous day's *auto-da-fé* of a hundred burned heretics. Is is not, however, a matter of indifference to us whether it's a *quiproquo*, or whether it's a colossal fantasy? The point is merely that the old man wants to speak his mind, to finally say out loud the things he has kept silent about for ninety years.'

'And the Captive says nothing either? Gazes at him, but says no word?'

'But that is how it must be in all such instances,' Ivan laughed again. 'The old man himself remarks to Him that He has not the right to add anything to what has already been said by Him in former times. If one cares to, one can see in that statement the most basic characteristic of Roman Catholicism, in my opinion, at least; it's as if they were saying: "It was all told by you to the Pope and so it is now all of it in the Pope's possession, and now we should appreciate it if you would stay away altogether and refrain from interfering for the time being, at any rate." That is the sense in which they not only speak but also write, the Jesuits, at least.
I've read such things in the works of their theologians. "Do

you have the right to divulge to us so much as one of the mysteries of the world from which you have come?" my old man asks Him, supplying the answer himself: "No, you do not, lest you add anything to what has already been said by you, and lest you take away from people the freedom you so stood up for when you were upon the earth. Anything new that you divulge will encroach upon people's freedom to believe, for it will look like a miracle and their freedom to believe was what mattered to you most even back then, fifteen hundred years ago. Was it not you who so often used to say back then: 'I want to make you free'? Well, but now you have seen those 'free' people," the old man suddenly adds with a thoughtful and ironic smile. "Yes, this task has cost us dearly," he continues, looking at him sternly, "but we have at last accomplished it in your name. For fifteen centuries we have struggled with that freedom, but now it is all over, and over for good. You don't believe that it is over for good? You look at me meekly and do not even consider me worthy of indignation? Well, I think you ought to be aware that now, and particularly in the days we are currently living through, those people are even more certain than ever that they are completely free, and indeed they themselves have brought us their freedom and have laid it humbly at our feet. But we were the ones who did that, and was that what you desired, that kind of freedom?" '

'Once again I don't understand,' Alyosha broke in. 'Is he being ironic, is he laughing?'

'Not at all. What he is doing is claiming the credit for himself and his kind for at last having conquered freedom and having done so in order to make people happy. "For only now" (he is talking about the Inquisition, of course) "has it become possible to think for the first time about people's happiness. Man is constituted as a mutineer; can mutineers ever be happy? You were given warnings," he says to Him, "you had plenty of warnings and instructions, but you did not obey them, you rejected the only path by which people could have been made happy, but fortunately when you left you handed over the task to us. You gave your promise, you sealed it with your word, you gave us the right to bind and loose, and so of course you cannot even dream of taking that right from us now. So why have you come to get in our way?" '

'I wonder if you could explain the meaning of that phrase: "you had plenty of warnings and instructions"?' Alyosha asked.

'Yes, well, that is exactly the point on which the old man wants to speak his mind.'

' "The terrible and clever Spirit, the Spirit of self-annihilation and nonexistence," the old man continues, "that great Spirit spoke with you in the wilderness, and we are told in the Scriptures that it 'tempted' you. Is that so? And would it be possible to say anything more true than those things which he made known to you in three questions and which you rejected, and which in the Scriptures are called 'temptations'? Yet at the same time, if ever there took place on the earth a truly thunderous miracle, it was on that day, the day of those three temptations. Precisely in the emergence of those three questions did the miracle lie. Were one to imagine, just for the sake of experiment and as an example, that those three questions put by the terrible Spirit had been lost without trace from the Scriptures and that it was necessary to reconstruct them, invent and compose them anew so they could again be entered in the Scriptures, and for this purpose to gather together all the sages of the earth—the rulers, the high priests, the scholars, the philosophers, the poets, and give them the task of inventing, composing three questions, but of such a kind that would not only correspond to the scale of the event but would also express, in three words, in but three human phrases, the entire future history of the world and mankind—then do you suppose that all the great wisdom of the earth, having united together, would be able to invent anything at all even remotely equivalent in power and depth to those three questions that were actually put to you that day by the mighty and clever Spirit in the wilderness? Why, by those very questions alone, by the sheer miracle of their emergence it is possible to gain the realization that one is dealing not with a fleeting human intelligence, but with one that is eternal and absolute. For it is as if in those three questions there is conjoined into a single whole and prophesied the entire subsequent history of mankind, there are manifested the three images in which all the unresolved historical contradictions of human nature throughout all the earth will coincide. Back then this was not as yet evident for the future was unknown, but now after the passage of fifteen centuries we can see that everything in those three questions was the product of such foresight and foreknowledge and was 31 so reasonable that it is no longer possible to add anything to them or to remove anything from them.

' "Decide for yourself who was right: You or the One who questioned You that day? Remember the first question, though not in literal terms, its sense was this: 'You want to go into the world and are going there with empty hands, with a kind of promise of freedom which they in their simplicity and inborn turpitude are unable even to comprehend, which they go in fear and awe of—for nothing has ever been more unendurable to man and human society than freedom! Look, you see those stones in that naked, burning hot wilderness? Turn them into loaves and mankind will go trotting after you like a flock, grateful and obedient, though ever fearful that you may take away your hand and that your loaves may cease to come their way.' But you did not want to deprive man of freedom and rejected the offer, for what kind of freedom is it, you reasoned, if obedience is purchased with loaves? You retorted that man lives not by bread alone, but are you aware that in the name of that same earthly bread the Earth Spirit will rise up against you and fight with you and vanquish you, and everyone will follow it, crying: 'Who is like unto this beast, he has given us fire from heaven!' Are you aware that centuries will pass, and mankind will proclaim with the lips of its wisdom and science that there is no crime and consequently no sin either, but only the hungry. 'Feed them, and then ask virtue of them!'—that is what will be inscribed upon the banner they will raise against you and before which your temple will come crashing down. In the place of your temple there will be erected a new edifice, once again a terrible Tower of Babel will be erected, and even though this one will no more be completed than was the previous one, but even so you would be able to avoid that new Tower and abbreviate the sufferings of the human beings by a thousand years, for after all, it is to us that they will come, when they have suffered for a thousand years with their Tower! Then they will track us down again under the ground, in the catacombs, hiding (for we shall again be persecuted and tortured), they will find us and cry to us: 'Feed us, for those who promised us fire from heaven have not granted it.' And then we shall complete their Tower, for it is he that feeds them who will complete it, and it is only we that shall feed them, in your name, and lie that we do it in your name. Oh, never, never will they feed themselves without us! No science will give them bread while yet they are free, but the end of it will be that they will bring us their freedom and place it at our feet and say to us: 'Enslave us if you will, but feed us.' At last they themselves will understand that freedom and earthly bread in sufficiency for all are unthinkable together, for never, never will they be able to share between themselves! They will also be persuaded that they will never be able to be free, because they are feeble, depraved, insignificant and mutinous. You promised them the bread of heaven, but, I repeat again, can it compare in the eyes of a weak, eternally depraved and eternally dishonourable human race with the earthly sort? And if in the name of the bread of heaven thousands and tens of thousands follow you, what will become of the millions and tens of thousand millions of creatures who are not strong enough to disdain the earthly bread for the heavenly sort? Or are the only ones you care about the tens of thousands of the great and the strong, while the remaining millions, numerous as the grains of sand in the sea, weak, but loving you, must serve as mere raw material for the great and the strong? No, we care about the weak, too. They are depraved and mutineers, but in the end they too will grow obedient. They will marvel at us and will consider us gods because we, in standing at their head, have consented to endure freedom and rule over them—so terrible will being free appear to them at last! But we shall say that we are obedient to you and that we rule in your name. We shall deceive them again, for we shall not let you near us any more. In that deception will be our suffering, for we shall be compelled to lie. That is the significance of the first question that was asked in the wilderness, and that is what you rejected in the name of freedom, which you placed higher than anything else. Yet in that question lay the great secret of this world. Had you accepted the 'loaves', you would have responded to the universal and age-old anguish of man, both as an individual creature and as the whole of mankind, namely the question: 'Before whom should one bow down?' There is for man no preoccupation more constant or more nagging than, while in a condition of freedom, quickly to find someone to bow down before. But man seeks to bow down before that which is already beyond dispute, so far beyond dispute that all human beings will instantly agree to a universal bowing-down before it. For the preoccupation of these miserable creatures consists not only in finding that

before which I or another may bow down, but in finding

something that everyone can come to believe in and bow down before, and that it should indeed be *everyone*, and that they should do it *all together*. It is this need for a *community* of bowing-down that has been the principal torment of each individual person and of mankind as a whole since the earliest ages. For the sake of a universal bowing-down they have destroyed one another with the sword. They have created gods and challenged one another: 'Give up your gods and come and worship ours or else death to you and to your gods!' And so it will be until the world's end, when even gods will vanish from the world: whatever happens, they will fall down before idols. You knew, you could not fail to know that peculiar secret of human nature, but you rejected the only absolute banner that was offered to you and that would have compelled everyone to bow down before you without dispute—the banner of earthly bread, and you rejected it in the name of freedom and the bread of heaven. Just take a look at what you did after that. And all of it again in the name of freedom! I tell you, man has no preoccupation more nagging than to find the person to whom that unhappy creature may surrender the gift of freedom with which he is born. But only he can take mastery of people's freedom who is able to set their consciences at rest. With bread you were given an undisputed banner: give bread and man will bow down, for nothing is more undisputed than bread, but if at the same time someone takes mastery of his conscience without your knowledge—oh, then he will even throw down your bread and follow the one who seduces his conscience. In that you were right. For the secret of human existence does not consist in living, merely, but in what one lives for. Without a firm idea of what he is to live for, man will not consent to live and will sooner destroy himself than remain on the earth, even though all around him there be loaves. That is so, but how has it worked out? Instead of taking mastery of people's freedom, you have increased that freedom even further! Or did you forget that peace of mind and even death are dearer to man than free choice and the cognition of good and evil? There is nothing more seductive for man than the freedom of his conscience, but there is nothing more tormenting for him, either. And so then in place of a firm foundation for the easing of the human conscience once and for all—you took everything that was exceptional, enigmatic and indeterminate, took everything that was beyond people's capacity to bear, and therefore acted as though you did not love them at all—and who was this? The one who had come to sacrifice his life for them! Instead of taking mastery of people's freedom, you augmented it and saddled the spiritual kingdom of man with it for ever. You desired that man's love should be free, that he should follow you freely, enticed and captivated by you. Henceforth, in place of the old, firm law, man was himself to decide with a free heart what is good and what is evil, with only your image before him to guide him—but surely you never dreamed that he would at last reject and call into question even your image and your truth were he to be oppressed by so terrible a burden as freedom of choice? They will exclaim at last that the truth is not in you, for it would have been impossible to leave them in more confusion and

torment than you did when you left them so many worries

and unsolvable problems. Thus, you yourself laid the foundation for the destruction of your own kingdom, and no one else should be blamed for it. And yet is that really what was offered you? There are three powers, only three powers on the earth that are capable of eternally vanquishing and ensnaring the consciences of those feeble mutineers, for their happiness—those powers are: miracle, mystery and authority. You rejected the first, the second and the third, and yourself gave the lead in doing so. When the wise and terrible Spirit set you on a pinnacle of the temple and said to you: 'If you would know whether you are the Son of God, then cast yourself down from hence, for it is written that the angels will take charge of him and bear him up, and he will not fall and dash himself to pieces—and then you will know if you are the Son of God, and will prove how much faith you have in your Father.' But having heard him through, you rejected his offer and did not give way and did not cast yourself down. Oh, of course, in that you acted proudly and magnificently, like God, but people, that weak, mutinying tribe—are they gods? Oh, that day you understood that by taking only one step, the step of casting yourself down, you would instantly have tempted the Lord and would have lost all faith in him, and would have dashed yourself to pieces against the earth which you had come to save, and the clever Spirit which had tempted you would rejoice. But, I repeat, are there many such as you? And could you really have supposed, even for a moment, that people would have the strength to resist such a temptation? Is human nature really of a kind as to be able to reject the miracle, and to make do, at such terrible moments of life, moments of the most terrible fundamental and tormenting spiritual questions, with only a free decision of the heart? Oh, you knew that your great deed would be preserved in the Scriptures, would attain to the depth of the ages and to the outermost limits of the earth, and you hoped that, in following you, man too would make do with God, not requiring a miracle. But you did not know that no sooner did man reject the miracle than he would at once reject God also, for man does not seek God so much as miracles. And since man is not strong enough to get by without the miracle, he creates new miracles for himself, his own now, and bows down before the miracle of the quack and the witchcraft of the peasant woman, even though he is a mutineer, heretic and atheist a hundred times over. You did not come down from the Cross when they shouted to you, mocking and teasing you: 'Come down from the Cross and we will believe that it is You.' You did not come down because again you did not want to enslave man with a miracle and because you thirsted for a faith that was free, not miraculous. You thirsted for a love that was free, not for the servile ecstasies of the slave before the might that has inspired him with dread once and for all. But even here you had too high an opinion of human beings, for of course, they are slaves, though they are created mutineers. Look around you and judge, now that fifteen centuries have passed, take a glance at them: which of them have you borne up to yourself? Upon my word, man is created weaker and more base than you supposed! Can he, can he perform the deeds of which you are capable? In respecting

38 him so much you acted as though you had ceased to have

compassion for him, because you demanded too much of him—and yet who was this? The very one you had loved more than yourself! Had you respected him less you would have demanded of him less, and that would have been closer to love, for his burden would have been lighter. He is weak and dishonourable. So what if now he mutinies against your power and is proud of his mutiny? This is the pride of a small boy, a schoolboy. These are little children, mutinying in class and driving out their teacher. But the ecstasy of the little boys will come to an end, it will cost them dearly. They will overthrow the temples and soak the earth in blood. But at last the stupid children will realize that even though they are mutineers, they are feeble mutineers, who are unable to sustain their mutiny. In floods of stupid tears they will at last recognize that the intention of the one who created them mutineers was undoubtedly to make fun of them. They will say this in despair, and their words will be blasphemy, which will make them even more unhappy, for human nature cannot endure blasphemy and in the end invariably takes revenge for it. Thus, restlessness, confusion and unhappiness—those are the lot of human beings now, after all that you underwent for the sake of their freedom! Your great prophet says in an allegorical vision that he saw all those who took part in the first resurrection and that of each tribe there were twelve thousand. But if there were so many of them, they cannot have been human beings, but gods. They had borne your Cross, they had borne decades in the hungry and barren wilderness, living on roots and locusts—and of course, it goes without saying that you may point with pride to those children of freedom, of a love that is free, of the free and magnificent sacrifice they have made in your name. Remember, however, that there were only a few thousand of them, and those were gods—but what about the rest? And in what way are the other weak human beings to blame for not having been able to bear the same things as the mighty? In what way is the weak soul to blame for not having the strength to accommodate such terrible gifts? And indeed, did you really only come to the chosen ones and for the chosen ones? But if that is so, then there is a mystery there and it is not for us to comprehend it. And if there is a mystery, then we were within our rights to propagate that mystery and teach them that it was not the free decision of their hearts and not love that mattered, but the mystery, which they must obey blindly, even in opposition to their consciences. And that was what we did. We corrected your great deed and founded it upon *miracle*, *mystery* and *authority*. And people were glad that they had once been brought together into a flock and that at last from their hearts had been removed such a terrible gift, which had brought them so much torment. Were we right, to teach and act thus, would you say? Did we not love mankind, when we so humbly admitted his helplessness, lightening his burden with love and allowing his feeble nature even sin, but with our permission? Why have you come to get in our way now? And why do you gaze at me so silently and sincerely with those meek eyes of yours? Why do you not get angry? I do not want your love, because I myself do not love you. And what is there I can conceal from you? Do you think I don't know who I'm talking to? What I have to say to you is all familiar to you already, I can read it in your eyes. And do you think I would conceal our secret from you? Perhaps it is my own lips that you want to hear it from—then listen: we are not with you, but with *him*, there is our secret! We have long been not with you, but with *him*, eight centuries now. It is now just eight centuries since we took from him that which you in indignation rejected, that final gift he offered you, when he showed you all the kingdoms of the world: we took from him Rome and the sword of Caesar and announced that we alone were the kings of the world, the only kings, even though to this day we have not succeeded in bringing our task to its complete fulfilment. But whose is the blame for that? Oh, this task is as yet only at its beginning, but it has begun. The world will have to wait for its accomplishment for a long time yet, and it will have to suffer much, but we shall reach our goal and shall be Caesars and then we shall give thought to the universal happiness of human beings. And yet even back then you could have taken the sword of Caesar. Why did you reject that final gift? Had you accepted that third counsel of the mighty Spirit, you would have supplied everything that man seeks in the world, that is: someone to bow down before, someone to entrust one's conscience to, and a way of at last uniting everyone into an undisputed, general consensual ant-heap, for the need of universal union is the third and final torment of human beings. Invariably mankind as a whole has striven to organize itself on a universal basis. Many great peoples have there been, and peoples with great histories, but the loftier those peoples, the more unhappy, for more acutely than others have they been conscious of the need for a universal union of human beings. The great conquerors, the Tamburlaines and Genghis Khans, hurtled like a whirlwind through the world, striving to conquer the universe, but even they, though they did so unconsciously, expressed the same great need of mankind for universal and general union. Had you accepted the world and the purple of Caesar, you would have founded a universal kingdom and given men universal peace. For who shall reign over human beings if not those who reign over their consciences and in whose hands are their loaves? Well, we took the sword of Caesar, and, of course, in taking it rejected you and followed *him*. Oh, centuries yet will pass of the excesses of the free intellect, of their science and anthropophagy, because, having begun to erect their Tower of Babel without us, they will end in anthropophagy. But then the beast will come crawling to our feet and lick them and sprinkle them with the bloody tears from his eyes. And we will sit upon the beast and raise the cup, and on it will be written: MYSTERY! But then and only then for human beings will begin the kingdom of peace and happiness. You are proud of your chosen ones, but all you have are chosen ones, and we shall bring rest to all. And there is more: how many of those chosen ones, of the mighty, who might have become chosen ones, at last grew tired of waiting for you, and have transferred and will yet transfer the energies of their spirits and the fervour of their hearts to a different sphere and end by raising their *free* banner against you. But it was you yourself who raised that banner. In our hands, though, everyone will 42 be happy and will neither mutiny nor destroy one another any more, as they do in your freedom, wherever one turns. Oh, we shall persuade them that they will only become free when they renounce their freedom for us and submit to us. And what does it matter whether we are right or whether we are telling a lie? They themselves will be persuaded we are right, for they will remember to what horrors of slavery and confusion your freedom has brought them. Freedom, the free intellect and science will lead them into such labyrinths and bring them up against such miracles and unfathomable mysteries that some of them, the disobedient and ferocious ones, will destroy themselves; others, disobedient and feeble, will destroy one another, while a third group, those who are left, the feeble and unhappy ones, will come crawling to our feet, and will cry out to us: 'Yes, you were right, you alone were masters of his secret, and we are returning to you, save us from ourselves.' Receiving loaves from us, of course, they will clearly see that what we have done is to take from them the loaves they won with their own hands in order to distribute it to them without any miracles, they will see that we have not turned stones into loaves, but truly, more than of the bread, they will be glad of the fact that they are receiving it from our hands! For they will be only too aware that in former times, when we were not there, the very loaves they won used merely to turn to stones in their hands, and yet now they have returned to us those very same stones have turned back to loaves again. All too well, all too well will they appreciate what it means to subordinate themselves to us once and for all! And until human beings understand that, they will be unhappy. Who contributed most of all to that

43

lack of understanding, tell me? Who split up the flock and scattered it over the unknown ways? But the flock will once more gather and once more submit and this time it will be for ever. Then we shall give them a quiet, reconciled happiness, the happiness of feeble creatures, such as they were created. Oh, we shall persuade them at last not to be proud, for you bore them up and by doing so taught them to be proud; we shall prove to them that they are feeble, that they are merely pathetic children, but that childish happiness is sweeter than all others. They will grow fearful and look at us and press themselves to us in their fear, like nestlings to their mother. They will marvel at us and regard us with awe and be proud that we are so powerful and so clever as to be able to pacify such a turbulent, thousand-million-headed flock. They will feebly tremble with fright before our wrath, their minds will grow timid, their eyes will brim with tears, like those of women and children, but just as lightly at a nod from us will they pass over into cheerfulness and laughter, radiant joy and happy children's songs. Yes, we shall make them work, but in their hours of freedom from work we shall arrange their lives like a childish game, with childish songs, in chorus, with innocent dances. Oh, we shall permit them sin, too, they are weak and powerless, and they will love us like children for letting them sin. We shall tell them that every sin can be redeemed as long as it is committed with our leave; we are allowing them to sin because we love them, and as for the punishment for those sins, very well, we shall take it upon ourselves. And we shall take it upon ourselves, and they will worship us as benefactors who have assumed re-

sponsibility for their sins before God. And they shall have no
secrets from us. We shall permit them or forbid them to live
with their wives or paramours, to have or not have
children—all according to the degree of their obedience—
and they will submit to us with cheerfulness and joy. The
most agonizing secrets of their consciences—all, all will they
bring to us, and we shall resolve it all, and they will attend
our decision with joy, because it will deliver them from the
great anxiety and fearsome present torments of free and individual decision. And all will be happy, all the millions of
beings, except for the hundred thousand who govern them.
For only, we, we, who preserve the mystery, only we shall be
unhappy. There will be thousands upon millions of happy
babes, and a hundred thousand martyrs who have taken upon
themselves the curse of the knowledge of good and evil. Quietly they will die, quietly they will fade away in your name
and beyond the tomb will find only death. But we shall preserve the secret and for the sake of their happiness will lure
them with a heavenly and eternal reward. For if there were
anything in the other world, it goes without saying that it
would not be for the likes of them. It is said and prophesied
that you will come and prevail anew, will come with your
chosen, your proud and mighty ones, but we will say that
they have saved only themselves, while we have saved all. It
is said that the whore who sits on the beast holding her MYS-
TERY will be disgraced, that the weak will rise up in mutiny
again, that they will tear her purple and render naked her
'desolate' body. But then I shall arise and draw your attention
to the thousands upon millions of happy babes, who know 45

not sin. And we, who for the sake of their happiness have taken their sins upon us, we shall stand before you and say: 'Judge us if you can and dare.' You may as well know that I am not afraid of you. You may as well know that I too was in the wilderness, that I too nourished myself on roots and locusts, that I too blessed the freedom with which you have blessed human beings, I too prepared myself to join the number of your chosen ones, the number of the strong and the mighty, with a yearning to 'fulfil the number'. But I came to my senses again and was unwilling to serve madness. I returned and adhered to the crowd of those who have *corrected your great deed*. I left the proud and returned to the humble for the sake of their happiness. What I say to you will come to pass, and our kingdom shall be accomplished. I tell you again: tomorrow you will see that obedient flock, which at the first nod of my head will rush to rake up the hot embers to the bonfire on which I am going to burn you for having come to get in our way. For if there ever was one who deserved our bonfire more than anyone else, it is you. Tomorrow I am going to burn you. *Dixi*.'"

Ivan paused. He had grown flushed from talking, and talking with passion; now that he had stopped, however, he suddenly smiled.

Alyosha, who had listened to him all this time without saying anything, though towards the end, in a state of extreme agitation, he had several times attempted to interrupt the flow of his brother's speech, but had evidently held himself in check, suddenly began to speak as though he had leapt

into motion.

'But . . . that is preposterous!' he exclaimed, turning red. 'Your poem is a eulogy of Jesus, not a vilification of him, as you intended it. And who will listen to you on the subject of freedom? That is a fine way, a fine way to understand it! That is not how it's understood in the Orthodox faith. That's Rome, and not even Rome completely, either, that isn't true—it's the worst elements in Catholicism, the inquisitors, the Jesuits! . . . And in any case, a fantastic character like your Inquisitor could not possibly have existed. What are these sins of human beings that have been taken by others upon themselves? Who are these bearers of mystery who have taken upon themselves some kind of curse for the sake of human happiness? Whoever heard of such people? We know the Jesuits, bad things are said of them, but they're not as they appear in your poem, are they? They're not at all like that, in no way like that . . . They are simply a Roman army for a future universal earthly kingdom, with an emperor— the Pontiff of Rome at their head . . . That is their ideal, but without any mysteries or exalted melancholy . . . The most straightforward desire for power, for sordid earthly blessings, for enslavement . . . like a future law of serf-ownership, with themselves as the owners . . . that's all they care about. Why, they probably don't even believe in God. Your suffering Inquisitor is only a fantasy . . .'

'Hold on, hold on,' Ivan said, laughing. 'What a temper you're in. A fantasy, you say—very well! All right, it's a fantasy. But wait a moment: do you really suppose that the whole of that Catholic movement of recent centuries is nothing but a desire for power in order to attain earthly comfort? 47

That wouldn't be something Father Paisy taught you, would it?'

'No, no, on the contrary, Father Paisy did actually once say something that was slightly similar to your idea . . . but of course it wasn't the same, not the same at all,' Alyosha suddenly remembered.

'A valuable piece of information, nevertheless, in spite of your, "not the same at all". The question I want to ask you is why have your Jesuits and inquisitors joined together for the sole purpose of attaining wretched material comfort? Why may there not be among them a single martyr, tormented by a great *Weltschmerz* and loving mankind? Look: suppose that out of all those who desire nothing but sordid material comfort there is just one—just one, like my aged Inquisitor—who has himself eaten roots in the wilderness and raged like one possessed as he conquered his flesh in order to make himself free and perfect, though all his life he has loved mankind and has suddenly had his eyes opened and seen that there is not much moral beatitude in attaining perfect freedom if at the same time one is convinced that millions of the rest of God's creatures have been stitched together as a mere bad joke, that they will never have the strength to cope with their freedom, that from pathetic mutineers there will never grow giants to complete the building of the Tower, that not for such geese did the great idealist dream of his harmony. Having understood all that, he returned and joined forces with . . . the clever people. Could that really not happen?'

48   'A fine lot of people he joined! How can one call them

clever?' Alyosha exclaimed, almost reckless in his passion. 'They have no intelligence, nor do they have any mysteries or secrets . . . Except perhaps atheism—that is their only secret. Your Inquisitor doesn't believe in God, that's his whole secret!'

'So what if even that is true? At last you've realized it! And indeed it is true, that is indeed the only secret, but is that not suffering, even for a man such as he, who has wasted his entire life on a heroic feat in the wilderness, and has not been cured of his love for mankind? In the decline of his days he becomes clearly persuaded that only the counsel of the terrible Spirit could in any way reconstitute in tolerable order the feeble mutineers, "imperfect, trial creatures, who were created as a bad joke". And lo, persuaded of this, he sees that it is necessary to proceed according to the indication of the clever Spirit, the terrible Spirit of death and destruction, and to such end accept deceit and falsehood and lead people consciously to death and destruction and deceive them moreover all of the way, so that they do not notice whither they are being led, so that at least on the way those pathetic blind creatures shall believe themselves happy. And note that it is deceit in the name of the One in whose ideal the old man had all his life so passionately believed! Is that not a misfortune? And even if there were only one such man at the head of this entire army, "thirsting for power for the sake of mere sordid earthly blessings", then would not one such man be enough to produce a tragedy? Not only that: one such man, standing at their head, would be enough in order to establish at last the whole guiding idea of the Roman cause with all its armies and Jesuits, the loftiest idea of that cause. I declare to you outright that I firmly believe that these unique men have never been hard to find among those who stand at the head of the movement. Who can say— perhaps there have been such unique men even among the Roman pontiffs? Who can say—perhaps that accursed old man who loved mankind with such a stubborn, original love exists even now in the form of a whole crowd of such unique old men and not by mere accident but as a secret alliance, formed long ago for the preservation of the mystery, for its preservation from feeble and unhappy human beings, in order to make them happy. That is certainly the case, and must be so. I fancy that even among the Masons there is something of the same sort of mystery at the basis of their movement and that the Catholics hate the Freemasons so much because they see them as rivals, a division of the unity of the idea, while there must be one flock and one shepherd . . . As a matter of fact, in defending my thesis like this, I feel like an author who is unable to withstand your criticism. Enough of this.'

'I think you are a Freemason yourself!' Alyosha suddenly let out. 'You don't believe in God,' he added, this time with extreme sorrow. It seemed to him, moreover, that his brother was gazing at him with mockery. 'How does your poem end?' he asked suddenly, looking at the ground. 'Or have we already had the end?'

'I was going to end it like this: when the Inquisitor falls silent, he waits for a certain amount of time to hear what his Captive will say in response. He finds His silence difficult to bear. He has seen that the Prisoner has listened to him all this time with quiet emotion, gazing straight into his eyes and evidently not wishing to raise any objection. The old man would like the Other to say something to him, even if it is bitter, terrible. But He suddenly draws near to the old man without saying anything and quietly kisses him on his bloodless, ninety-year-old lips. That is His only response. The old man shudders. Something has stirred at the corners of his mouth; he goes to the door, opens it and says to Him: 'Go and do not come back . . . do not come back at all . . . ever . . . ever!' And he releases him into "the town's dark streets and squares." The Captive departs.'

'And the old man?'

'The kiss burns within his heart, but the old man remains with his former idea.'

'And you along with him, you too?' Alyosha exclaimed sadly. Ivan laughed.

'Oh, Alyosha, why, you know, it's nonsense—it's just an incoherent *poema* by an incoherent student who has never so much as put two lines of verse to paper. Why are you taking it so seriously? Surely you don't think that now I shall go straight there, to the Jesuits, in order to join the crowd of people who are correcting His great deed? Oh Lord, what do I care about that? I mean, I told you: all I want to do is hold out until I'm thirty, and then—dash the cup to the floor!'

'And the sticky leaf-buds, and the beloved tombs, and the blue sky, and the woman you love? How are you going to live, what are you going to love them with?' Alyosha exclaimed sadly. 'With a hell like that in your breast and your head, is it possible? No, of course you're going to join them . . . and if you don't, you'll kill yourself, you won't be able to endure!'

'There is a power that can endure everything!' Ivan said, with a cold, ironic smile now.

'What power?'

'The Karamazovian power . . . the power of Karamazovian baseness.'

'You mean, to drown in depravity, to crush the life from your soul in corruption, is that it, is that it?'

'Possibly that too . . . Only perhaps when I'm thirty, I shall escape, and then . . .'

'But how will you escape? With what means will you escape? With your ideas it's impossible.'

'Again, the Karamazovian way.'

'So that "all things are lawful"? All things are lawful, is that what you mean, is that it?'

Ivan frowned and suddenly turned strangely pale.

'Ah, you've got hold of the little remark I made yesterday at which Miusov took such offence . . . and which brother Dmitry was so naïve as to butt in and repeat?' he said, smiling a crooked smile. 'Yes, perhaps: "all things are lawful", since the remark has been made. I do not disown it. And dear Mitya's version of it is not so bad, either.'

Alyosha stared at him without saying anything.

'In leaving, brother, I had imagined that in all the world I have only you,' Ivan said suddenly, with unexpected emotion, 'but now I see that in your heart there is no room for me, my 52 dear hermit. I do not disown the formula "all things are lawful", but, I mean, are you going to disown me because of it—eh? eh?'

Alyosha rose, walked over to him, and without saying anything kissed him quietly on the lips.

'Literary thieving!' Ivan exclaimed, suddenly passing into a kind of ecstasy. 'You stole that from my *poema!* But never mind, I thank you. Come on, Alyosha, let us go, it is time both for you and for me.'

They went outside, but paused by the entrance to the inn.

'Look, Alyosha,' Ivan pronounced in a resolute voice. 'If I am indeed capable of loving the sticky leaf-buds, then I shall love them at the mere memory of you. It is enough for me that you are somewhere here, and I shan't yet lose my will to live. Is that enough for you? If you like, you may take it as a confession of love. But now you must go to the right and I to the left—and enough, do you hear, enough. That is to say that if it proves that I do not leave tomorrow (though it seems to me that I most certainly shall) and we were again to meet somehow, then I want you not to say another word to me on all these subjects. I earnestly request you. And concerning brother Dmitry I also particularly request that you not even so much as mention him to me ever again,' he added in sudden irritation. 'It's all settled and decided, isn't it? And in exchange for that, I for my part will also give you a certain promise: when I attain the age of thirty and want to "dash the cup to the floor" then, wherever you are, I shall come once again to discuss things with you . . . even if it's from America, I shall have you know. I shall come specially. It will be very interesting to set eyes on you at that time: 53

what will you be like? You see, it's quite a solemn sort of promise. And indeed it may well be that we are saying goodbye for seven, for ten years. Well, go to your *Pater Seraphicus* now, after all, he is dying; if he dies in your absence you may well be angry at me for having kept you back. Goodbye, kiss me once more—like that—and go . . .'

Ivan suddenly turned and went his way, without looking round this time. It resembled the manner in which brother Dmitry had left Alyosha the day before, though then the mood had been quite different. This strange little observation flashed, like an arrow, through Alyosha's sad mind, sad and sorrowful at that moment. He waited for a bit as he watched his brother go. For some reason he suddenly noticed that brother Ivan walked with a kind of sway and that, seen from behind, his right shoulder looked lower than his left. Never had he observed this previously. Suddenly, however, he also turned and set off almost at a run in the direction of the monastery. It was by now getting very dark, and he felt a sense that was almost one of fear; something new was growing within him, something he was unable to account for. The wind rose again, as it had done yesterday, and the ancient pine trees soughed darkly around him as he entered the hermitage woods. He was almost running. 'Pater Seraphicus'—that name, he had taken it from somewhere—where?—flashed through Alyosha's brain. 'Ivan, poor Ivan, and when will I see you again . . . Here is the hermitage, O Lord! Yes, yes, it is him, it is *Pater Seraphicus*, he will save me . . . from him and for ever!'

Later on, several times in his life, he recollected that moment with great bewilderment, wondering how he could suddenly, having only just parted with Ivan, so completely forgot his brother Dmitry, who that morning, only a few hours ago, he had determined to track down, vowing not to return without having done so, even if it meant he could not go back to the monastery that night.

PENGUIN 60s

are published on the occasion of Penguin's 60th anniversary

LOUISA MAY ALCOTT · *An Old-Fashioned Thanksgiving and Other Stories*

HANS CHRISTIAN ANDERSEN · *The Emperor's New Clothes*

J. M. BARRIE · *Peter Pan in Kensington Gardens*

WILLIAM BLAKE · *Songs of Innocence and Experience*

GEOFFREY CHAUCER · *The Wife of Bath and Other Canterbury Tales*

ANTON CHEKHOV · *The Black Monk* and *Peasants*

SAMUEL TAYLOR COLERIDGE · *The Rime of the Ancient Mariner*

COLETTE · *Gigi*

JOSEPH CONRAD · *Youth*

ROALD DAHL · *Lamb to the Slaughter and Other Stories*

ROBERTSON DAVIES · *A Gathering of Ghost Stories*

FYODOR DOSTOYEVSKY · *The Grand Inquisitor*

SIR ARTHUR CONAN DOYLE · *The Man with the Twisted Lip*
    and *The Adventure of the Devil's Foot*

RALPH WALDO EMERSON · *Nature*

OMER ENGLEBERT (TRANS.) · *The Lives of the Saints*

FANNIE FARMER · *The Original 1896 Boston Cooking-School Cook Book*

EDWARD FITZGERALD (TRANS.) · *The Rubáiyát of Omar Khayyám*

ROBERT FROST · *The Road Not Taken and Other Early Poems*

GABRIEL GARCÍA MÁRQUEZ · *Bon Voyage, Mr President and Other Stories*

NIKOLAI GOGOL · *The Overcoat* and *The Nose*

GRAHAM GREENE · *Under the Garden*

JACOB AND WILHELM GRIMM · *Grimm's Fairy Tales*

NATHANIEL HAWTHORNE · *Young Goodman Brown and Other Stories*

O. HENRY · *The Gift of the Magi and Other Stories*

WASHINGTON IRVING · *Rip Van Winkle* and *The Legend of Sleepy Hollow*

HENRY JAMES · *Daisy Miller*

V. S. VERNON JONES (TRANS.) · *Aesop's Fables*

JAMES JOYCE · *The Dead*

GARRISON KEILLOR · *Truckstop and Other Lake Wobegon Stories*

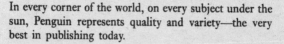